A
A

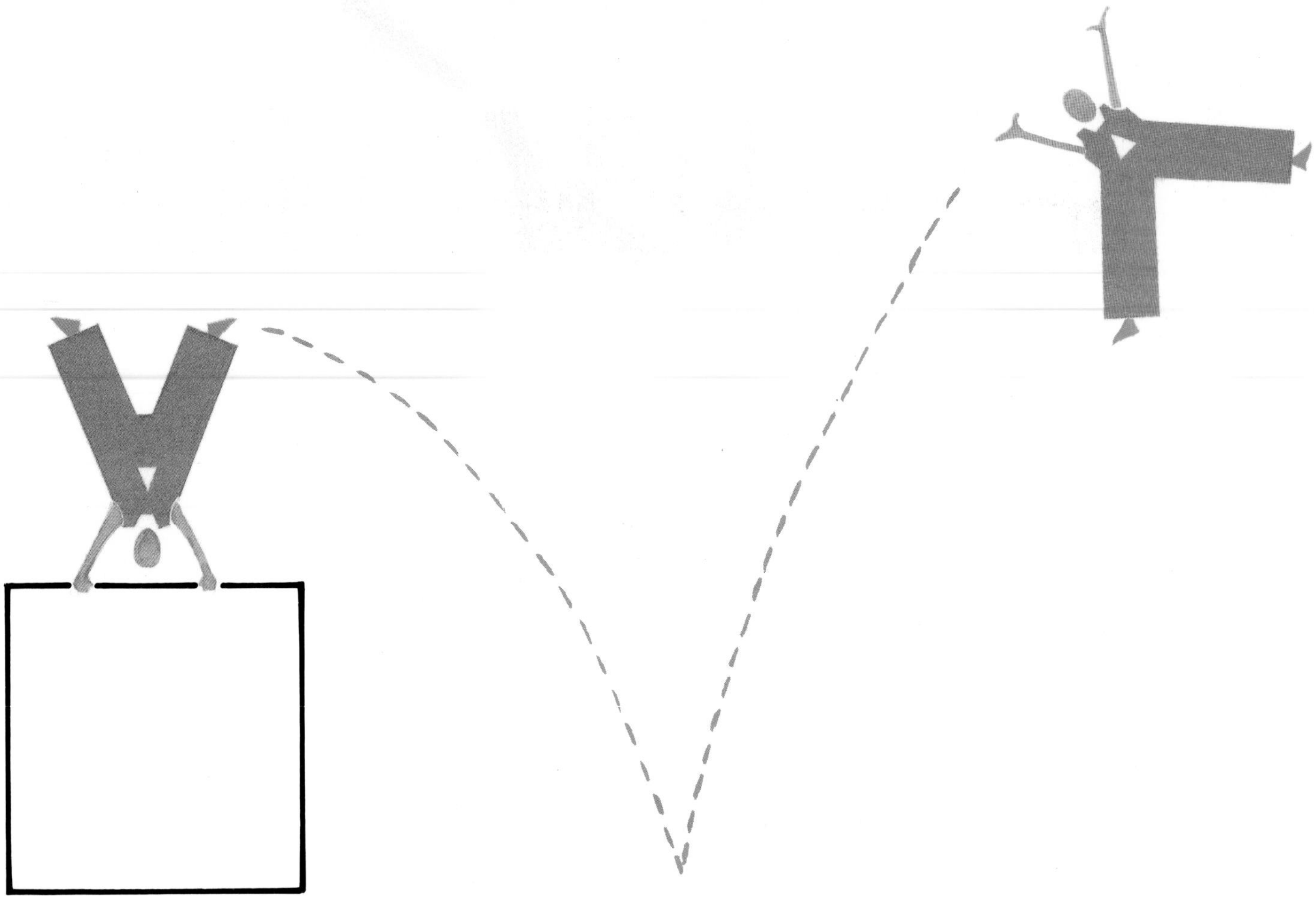

[redacted]

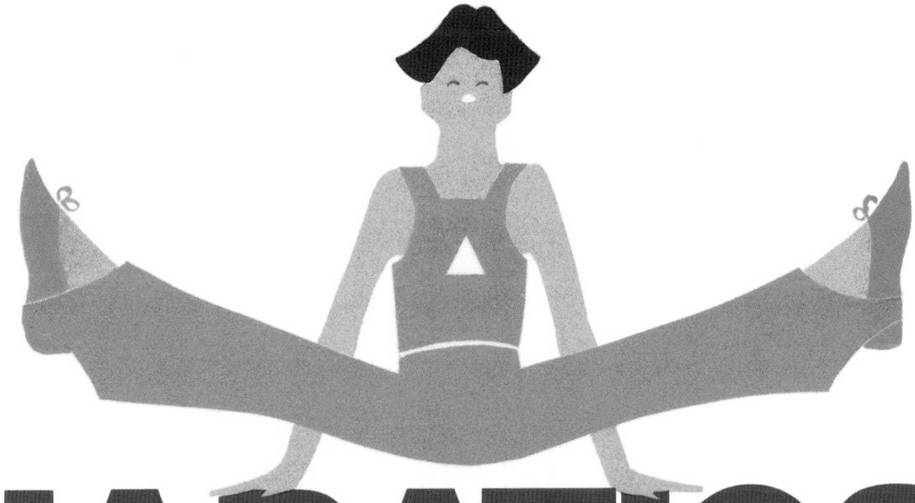

ALPHABATICS

Suse MacDonald

Aladdin Paperbacks

Aa

Ark

Bb

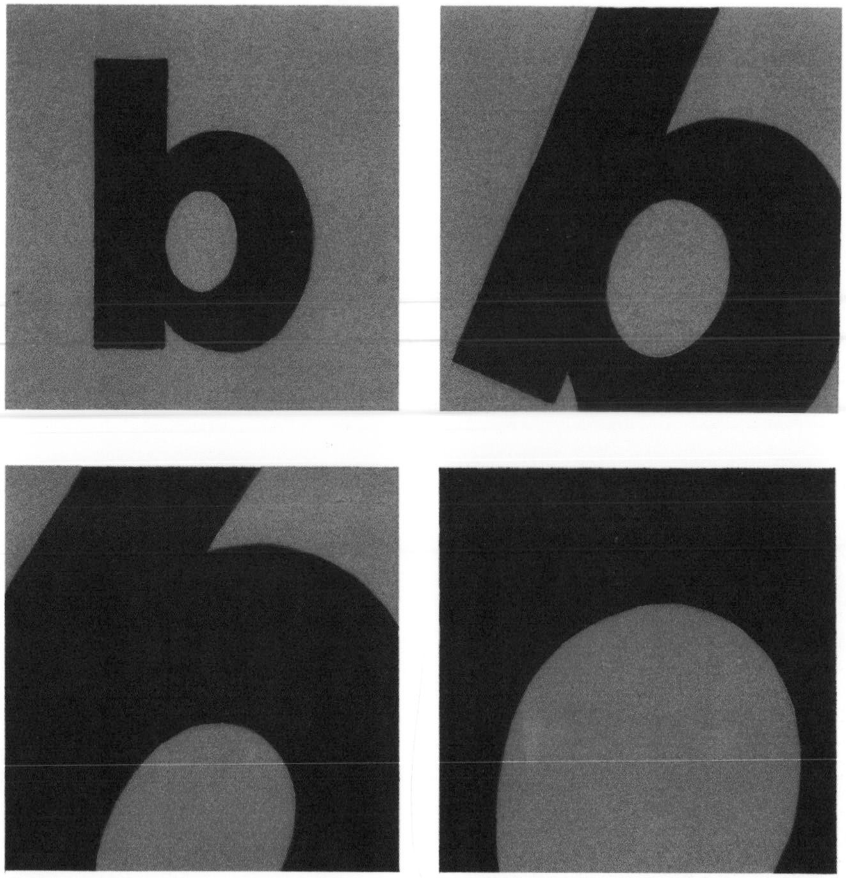

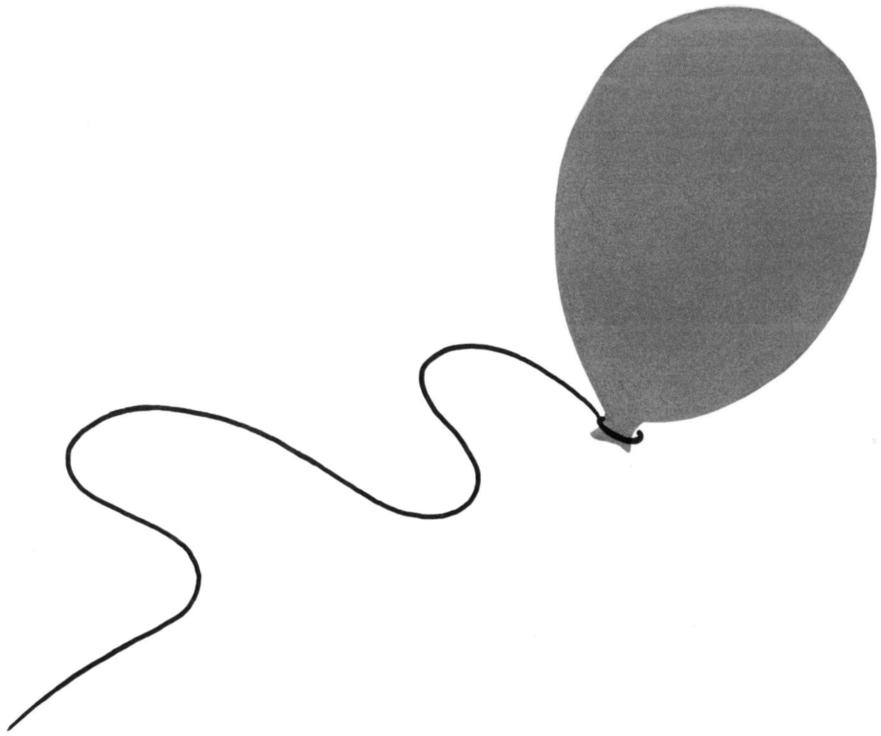

balloon

Cc

Clown

Dd

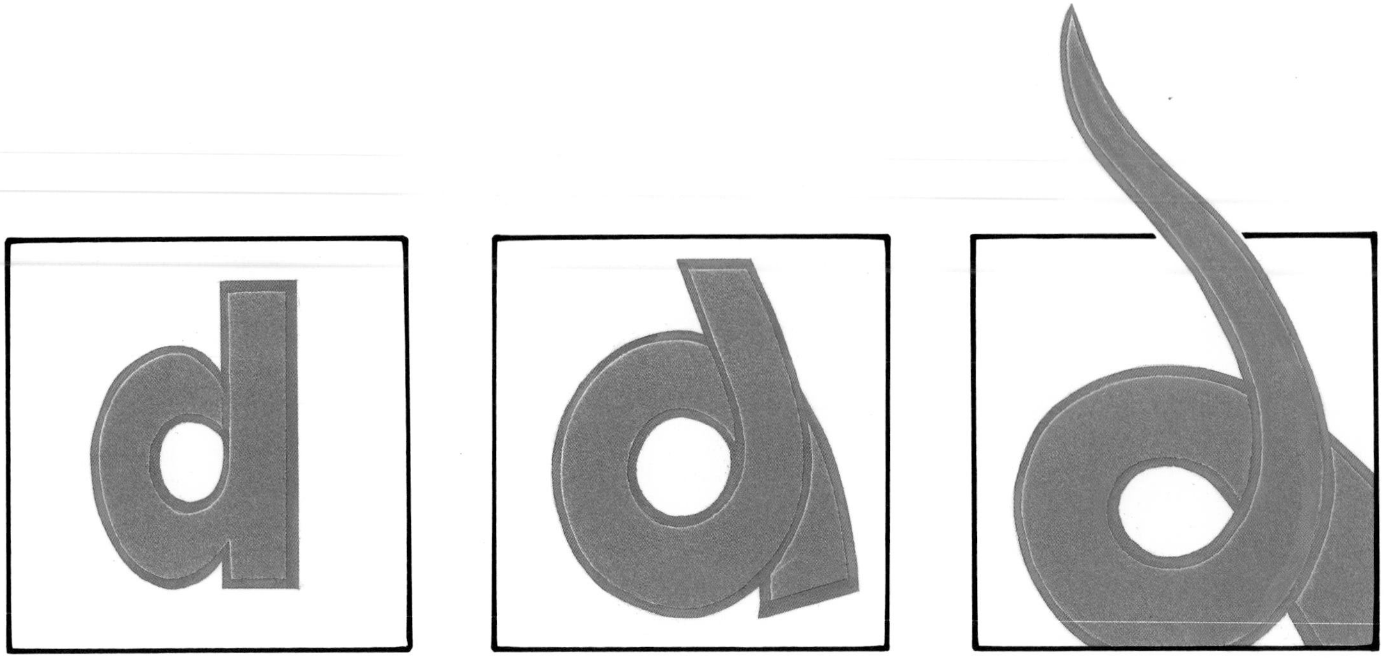

dragon

Ee

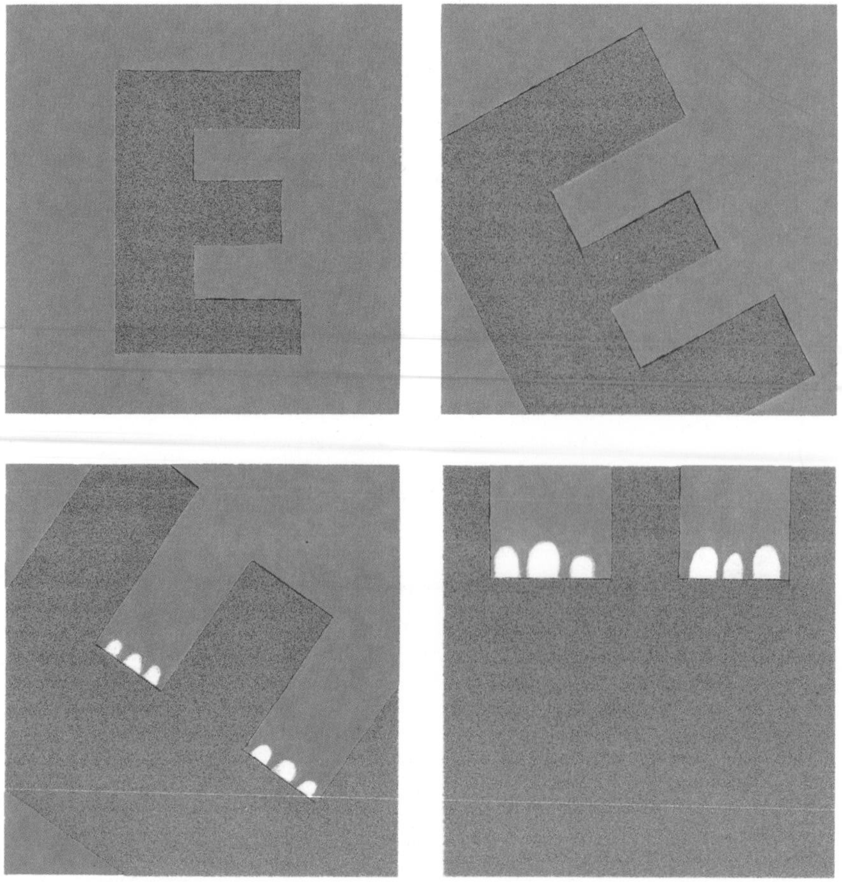

Elephant

Ff

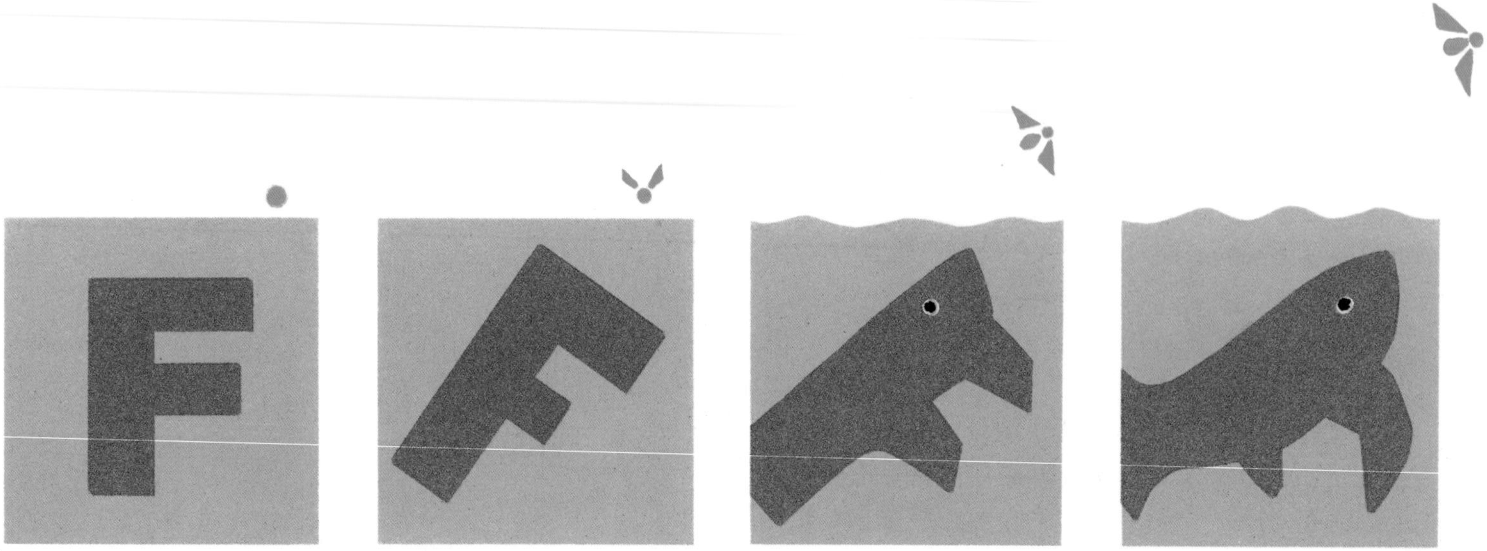

Fish

Gg

Giraffe

Hh

house

Ii

insect

Jj

jack-in-the-box

Kk

Kite

LI

Lion

Mm

mustache

Nn

nest

Oo

owl

Pp

Plane

Qq

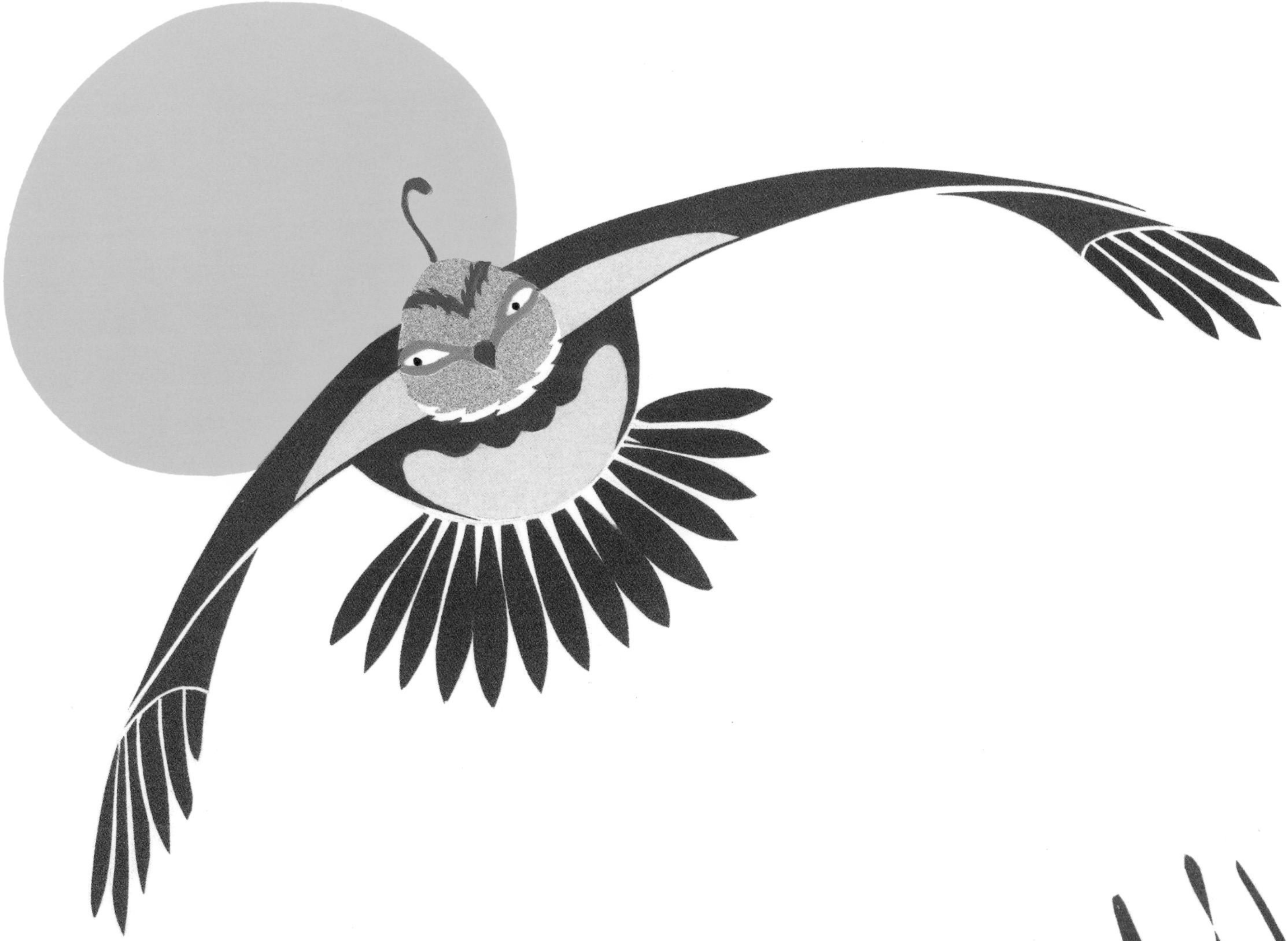

Quail

Rr

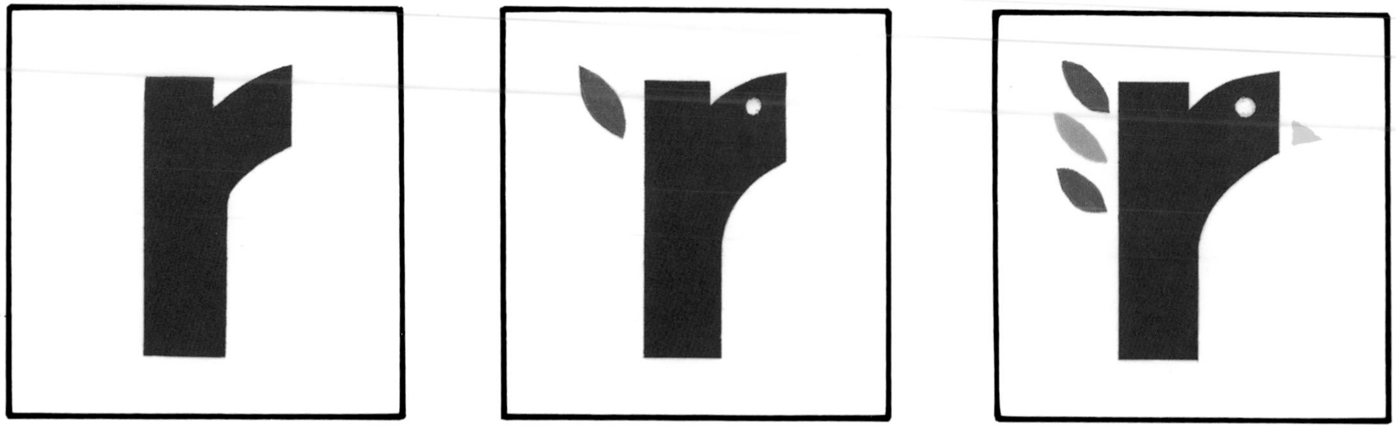

rooster

Ss

Swan

Tt

Tree

Uu

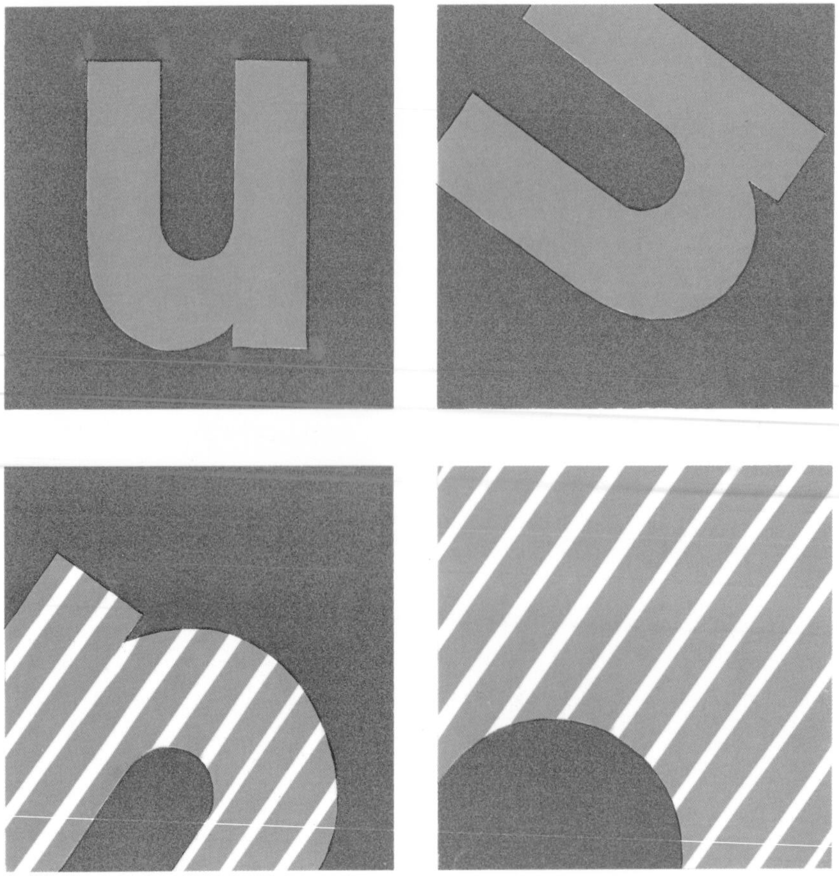

umbrella

Vv

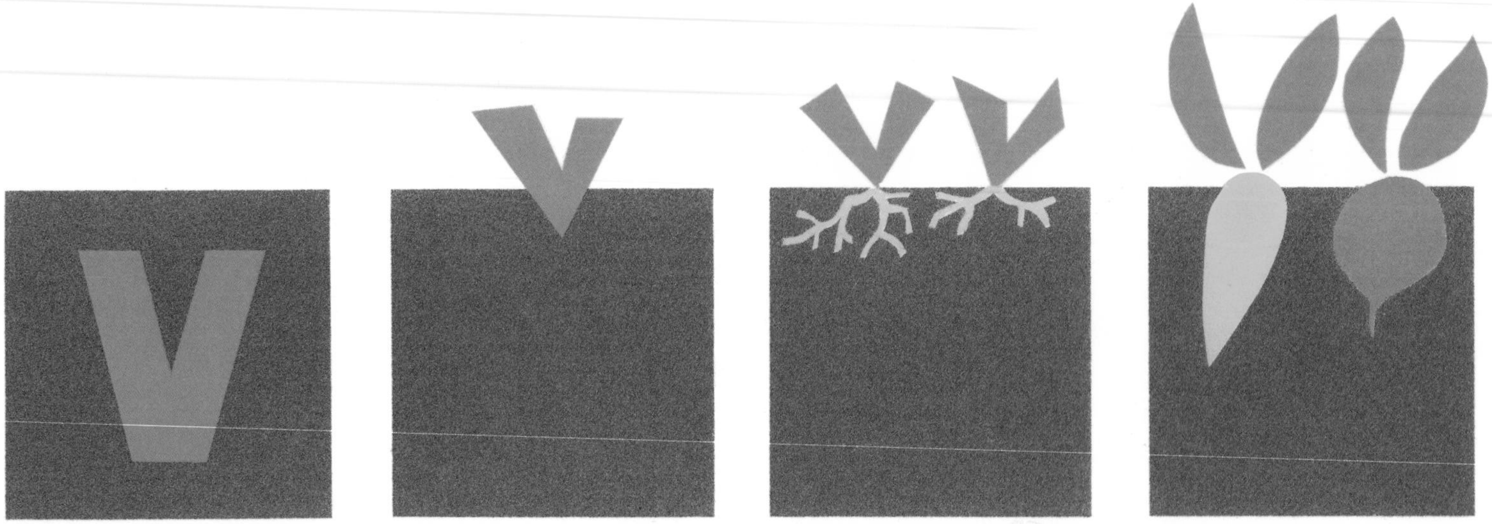

Vegetables

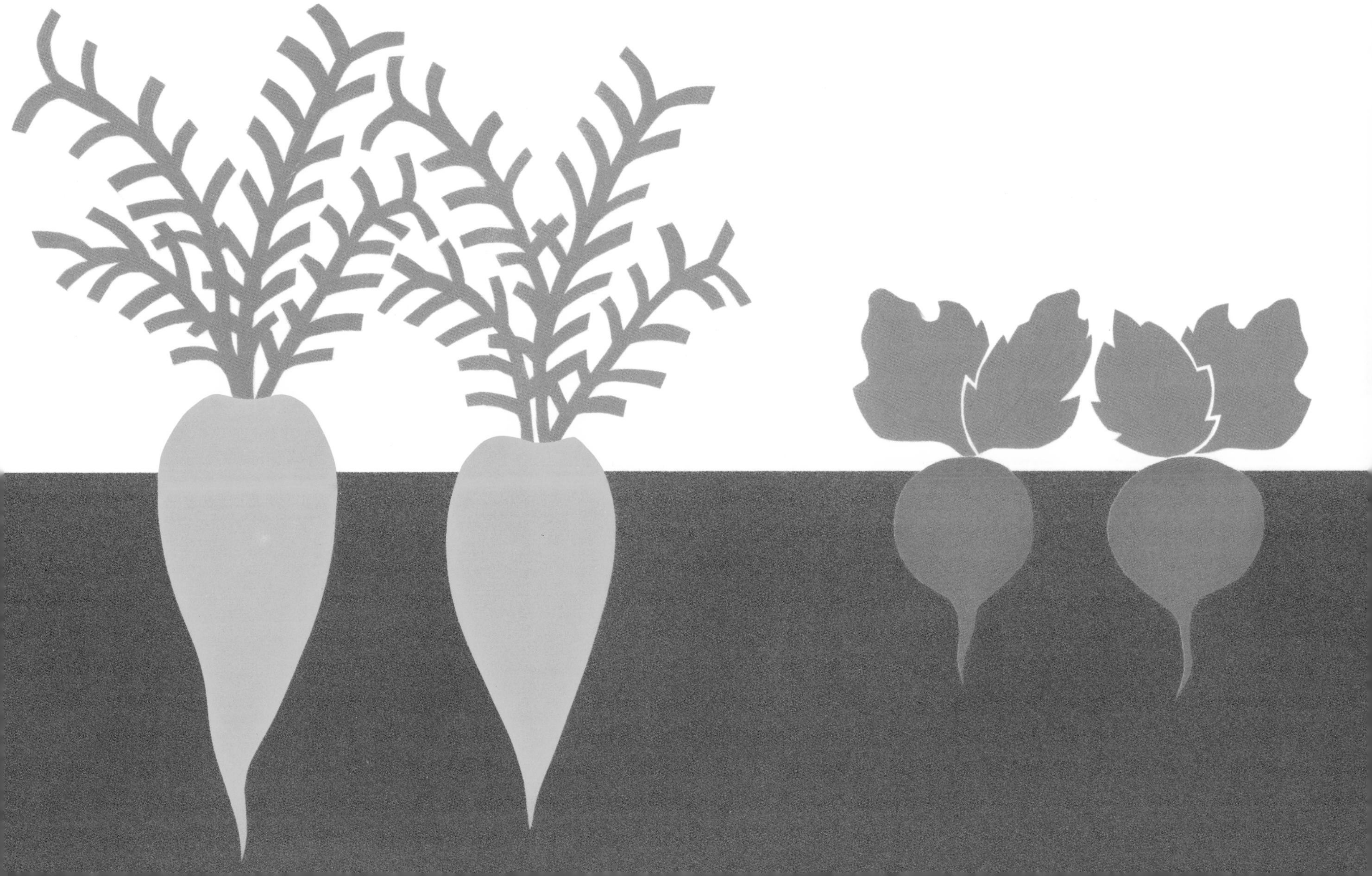

Ww

Whale

Xx

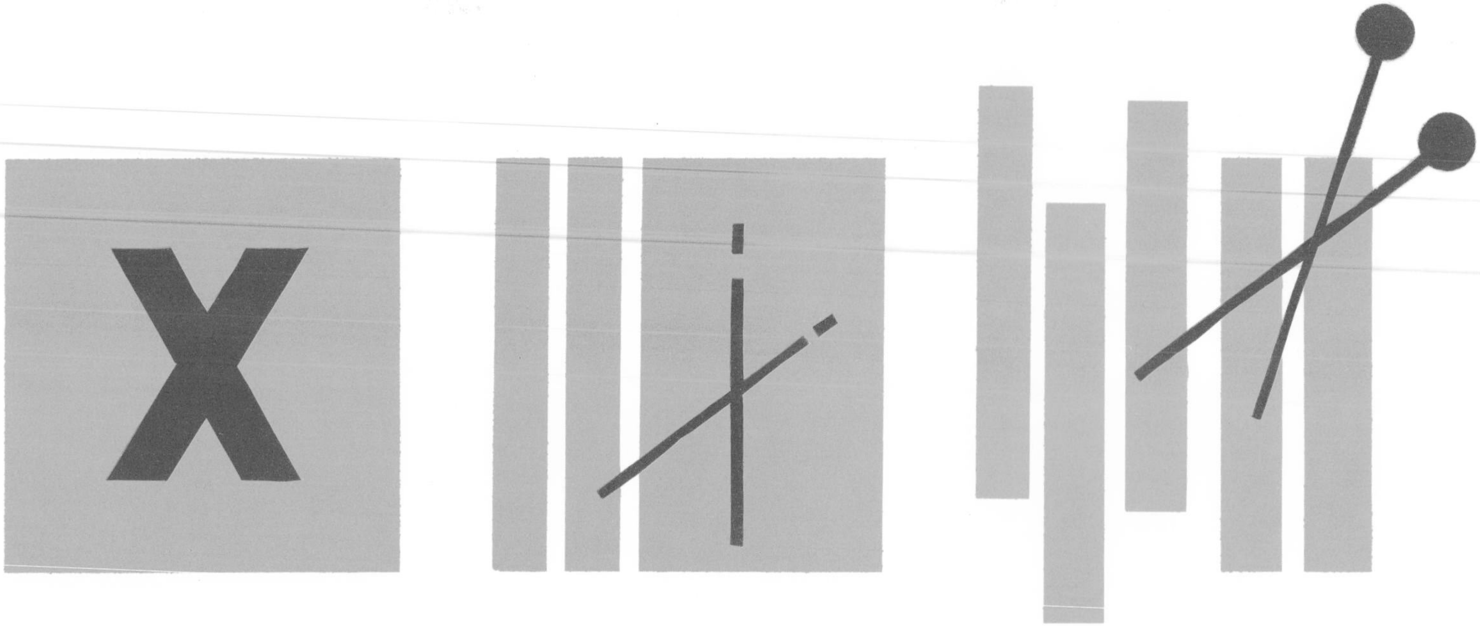

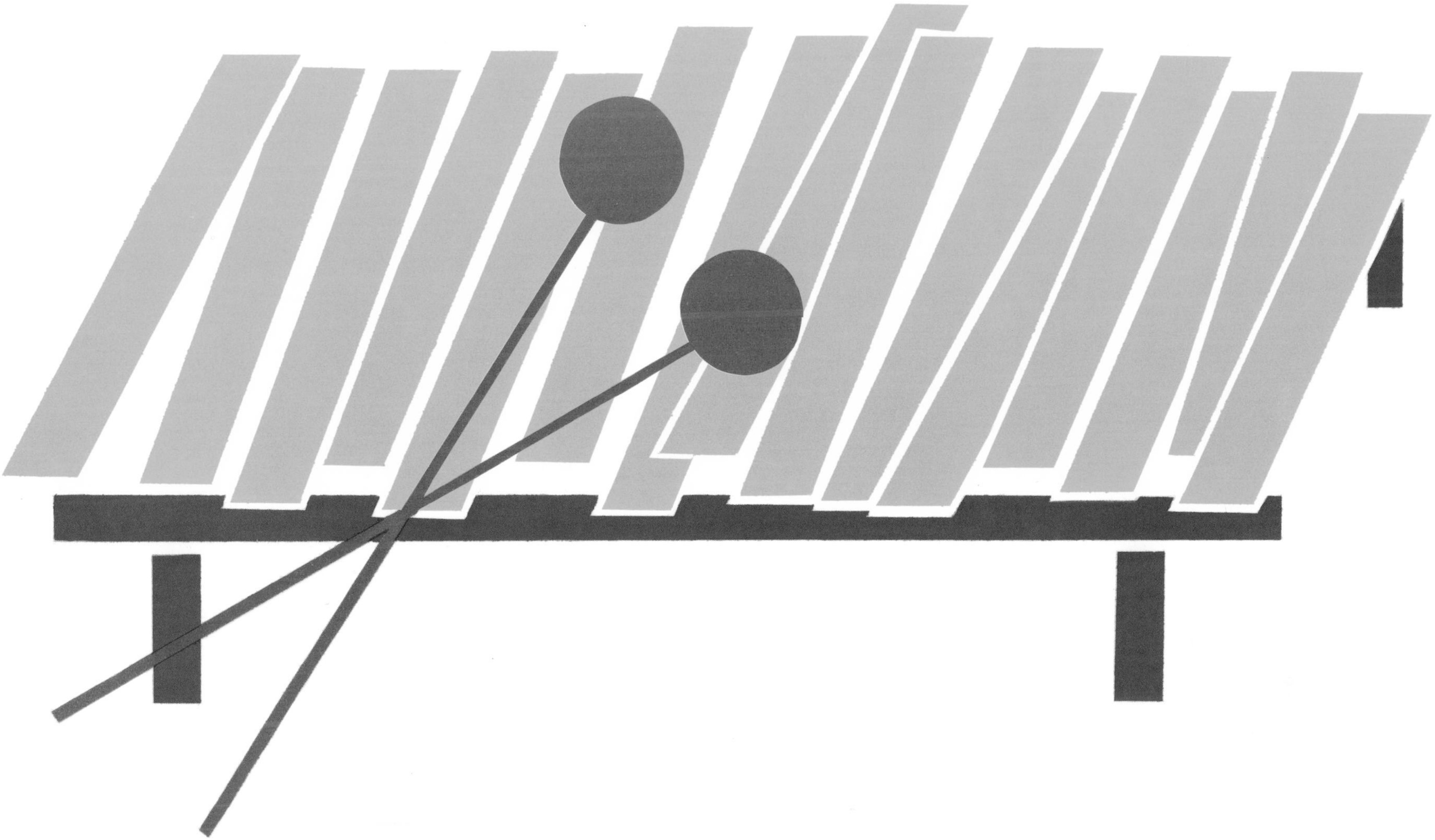

Xylophone

Yy

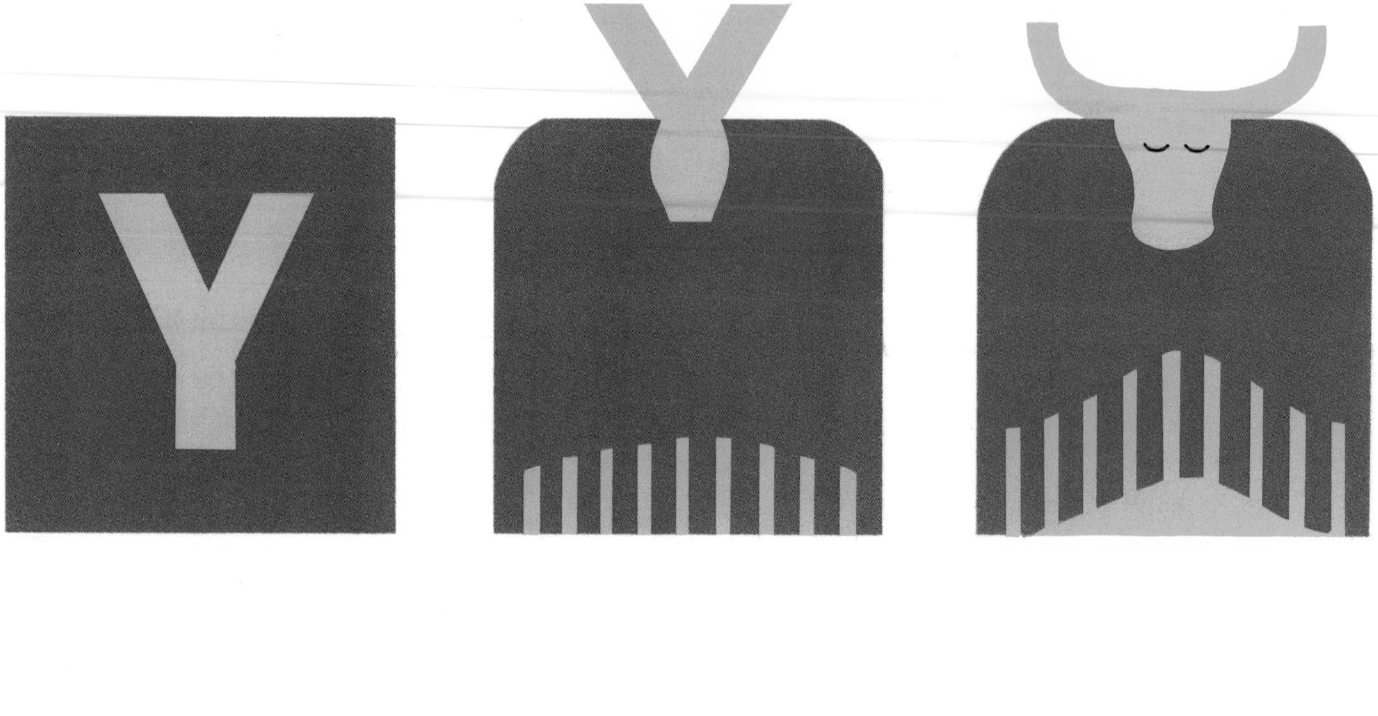

Yak

Zz

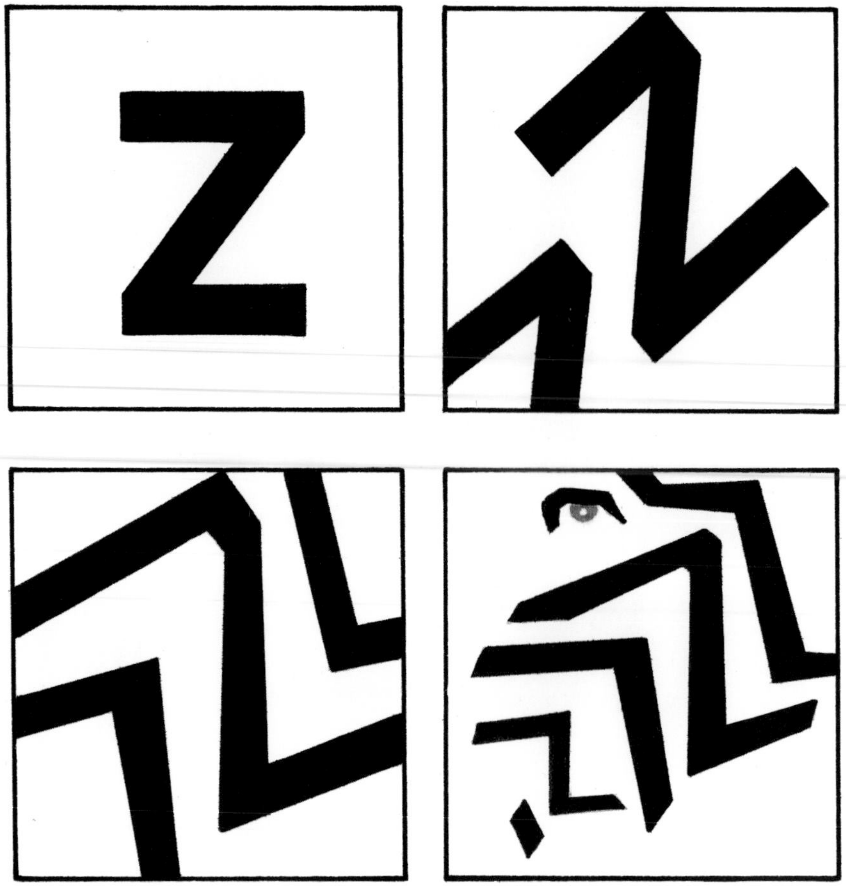

Zebra

For Stuart, with special thanks to Susan and Deborah

Aladdin Paperbacks. An imprint of Simon & Schuster Children's Publishing Division, 1230 Avenue of the Americas, New York, NY 10020. First Aladdin Paperbacks edition, 1992. Also available in a hardcover edition from Simon & Schuster Books for Young Readers. Printed in Hong Kong. 10 9 8 7 6 5

Library of Congress Cataloging-in-Publication Data MacDonald, Suse. Alphabatics / by Suse MacDonald. — 1st Aladdin Books ed. p. cm. Originally published: New York : Bradbury Press, 1986. Summary: The letters of the alphabet are transformed and incorporated into twenty-six illustrations, so that the hole in "b" becomes a balloon and "y" turns into the head of a yak. ISBN 0-689-71625-7 1. English Language—Alphabet—Juvenile literature. [1. Alphabet.] I. Title. PE1155.M3 1992 [E]—dc20 91-38497